In the Dead of Night

Det. Lt. Harvey Plains had it with police work in Fairfield, Texas. He had to get away, but any nearby state was the same. Cpt. Vernor was just leaving the station, after telling Harve that the judge threw out his case against Oswald and Gene Malcolm.

That was proven ten times over! They killed Jorge and Sylvia Gomez in as heinous a way as he had ever come across!

The Malcolms were rich rednecks. The Gomez family was Latino. He should have known.

He sighed and e-mailed Carter Amos, a friend who was on a long vacation in the Caribbean. He got a reply in less than two minutes.

Hi, Harve – Still want to get the hell out of the rat race there? Maybe work on something a lot different?

Come to Tinta Verde Island! This is right down your line! It could lead to you having a permanent job in Heaven!

He thought about it, sent his reply, and started writing his resignation. This time, he was going through with it.

Contents

About the author

CD Moulton has traveled extensively over much of the world both in the music business, where he was a rock guitarist, songwriter and arranger and in an import/export business. He has been everything from a bar owner to auto salvage (junkyard) manager, longshoreman to high steel worker, orchid grower to landscaper, tropical fish farmer to commercial fisherman. He started writing books in 1983 and has published more than 350 books as of January 1, 2023. His most popular books to date are about research with orchids, though much of his science fiction and fantasy work has proven popular. He wrote the CD Grimes, PI series, and the Det. Nick Storie series, Clint Faraday series, and many other works.

He now resides in Gualaca, Chiriqui, Panamá, where he writes books, plays music with friends, does research with orchids and medicinal plants. He has lately become involved in fighting for the rights of the indigenous people, who are among his closest friends, and in fighting the extreme corruption in the courts and police in Panamá.

He offers the free e-book, *Fading Paradise*, that explains what he has been through because of the corruption.

CD is the discoverer of the Chadam Protocol for curing cancer.

Facebook page Ambrosia peruviana for cancer.

In the Dead of Night

<u>*Disgust*</u>

Det. Lt. Harvey Plains had it with police work in Fairfield, Texas. He had to get away, but any nearby state was the same. Cpt. Vernor was just leaving the station, after telling Harve that the judge threw out his case against Oswald and Gene Malcolm for the torture murders.

That was proven ten times over! They killed Jorge and Sylvia Gomez in as heinous a way as he had ever come across! They were tied, beaten, cut, burned ... it was truly a sickening, disgusting murder scene.

The Malcolms were rich rednecks. They owned a few thousand acres of mostly cattle land. They seemed to be well above the law. Harve had actually seen them unloading some very suspicious packages from a small plane on their private runway.

He couldn't report that. He wasn't, technically, in a legal position to be on the property. He was acting on information, on his own. He knew that reporting it would end up with him being fired or worse. Nothing would be done.

This, rather obviously, extended to murder.

The Gomez family was Latino. He should have known.

He sighed and e-mailed Carter Amos, a PI who was working with some kind of government thing, and a friend who was on a long (probably working) vacation in the Caribbean. He got a reply in less than two minutes.

Hi, Harve – Still want to get the hell out of the rat race there? Maybe work on something a lot different? It's part of police work, but you won't have to put up with the bullshit you do there. You can't be bribed or intimidated, and almost nobody would try that here, under the circumstances. It could be tied to your situation. Probably is.

Come to Tinta Verde Island! This is right down your line! It could lead to you having a permanent job in Heaven!

He thought about it, sent his reply, and started writing his resignation. This time, he was going through with it.

He would be fired or worse for even bringing the charges against a Malcolm. This would thwart their plan to get intimidating publicity through some manipulated scheme. "Cross us, and see what you get!" was going to backfire. He was going to "get" to live on some tropical island!

He finished the short form and filled out the back with his reasons.

I have been on this force for four and a half years. I have worked from rookie to DLt in that time. My record is excellent. I cannot, in clear conscience, continue in a situation where certain people are above the law. The deterioration in law enforcement here leaves me no other honorable option. I took an oath, and I consider my word to be my personal worth. If my word, much less an oath, is broken, I am a piece of shit. Which I AM NOT.

He signed it. It was effective as of noon tomorrow.

He handed the form to Annette Birns, Vernor's private secretary, who looked shocked. He waved, and went to his cruiser.

His first stop was the Gomez place, where the family was is shock, themselves. They expected the Malcolms to get minimum on a reduced charge. They didn't expect them to get the case entirely thrown out.

"My brother works for Gaines Import Motors," Emilio Gomez V. said tiredly. "Judge Evans has a brand new BMW, paid for by George Sanders, lawyer for the Malcolm Dairies. That says it all, amigo."

"Well, I'm just wondering about things and stopped by to say I'm sorry for the way you're being treated. I was sort of wondering if it was time to have the oppressed people here protest the total lack of justice they receive at the hands of that crooked judge and such as the Malcolm brothers. Why, exactly those people are going to have a late evening at the Malcolm Grand tonight at ten o'clock to celebrate the court decision in their favor. They have also requested that the police surveillance is complete, as they fear the Latinos here might feel ... revengeful.

"I was wondering what could happen if, just coincidentally, the Latinos staged a march in protest on the other side of town that required all police officers to respond. It would leave those upstanding pillars of the community without protection! I mean, a terrorist attack at just that time ... I don't want to think about it!

"Well, amigos, I guess we'll not be seeing each other for awhile. I've resigned from the police here. I'm going on a vacation in the Caribbean, to an island called Tinta Verde. It's supposed to be a real paradise!"

"Isla Tinta Verde?! Madre de dios! El Diablo esta!" Maria cried. She crossed herself.

"What?" Harve asked. "You know Tinta Verde?"

"Si," Emilio answered. "We know of it. Maria says the devil is there, and, if the stories are true, he might be there.

"Por favor, amigo! Do not go! The Malcolm family owns a sugar plantation there and have piñas!"

"Then I'm going. I'm disgusted with the Malcolms and their power here. I can picture what it's like where they have even more power."

Harvey sighed, looked at the clock, and got up. He had spent until one AM at a protest by the Latino community, as had everyone in the police here and several state marshals, but it had remained peaceful, for the most part. He was one of the two officers locally and all state marshals who advised it would be very unwise to make any arrests. It was a peaceful demonstration, and arrests could bring national attention and federal intervention. Vernor argued that he didn't care. They had to be kept in their place.

Glen Forbes, a news reporter for local TV, got a video of him making that statement. He told the marshals, if any arrest was made, that video would go viral on the internet.

The rest of the night was Vernor trying to get his fat out of the fire, mostly by saying he didn't say what he said.

He put on the coffee pot and scrambled some eggs and put two slices in the toaster, He downed the eggs and toast, had a cuppa, and did the SSS routine, then turned on the 6:00 AM news.

"... couldn't find anyone who saw or heard anything. 'It can't be considered a terrorist attack, because they want publicity, and we didn't know anything about it until the floor manager went into the private ball room and found the bodies,' Police Captain Arnold Vernor stated.

"It seems that Oswald and Eugene Malcolm and their father Oscar Malcolm, along with Judge Robert Evans and a chauffeur, Andy "Snake" Johns and bartender Ted Felsom were dining in the ballroom when someone, probably several, people entered and slew all of them with machetes or other large knives.

"Captain Vernor says the investigation will be intense. No motive is apparent for the killings in the dead of night, even if it was in a hotel ball-room.

"Well, Connie! I would think the fact that machetes were used tells us a lot, don't you?"

"It would, Beth, except all the Latinos from this area were at a protest at the time, as confirmed by our reporters at the scene of the protest.

"My sources say there were a lot of drugs, mostly cocaine, found in the room. The Malcolms own land in Mexico, Nicaragua, Costa Rica, Panamà, Peru, Ecuador and Colombia, as well as several islands south of Cuba.

"DUH!"

"That is interesting! Do you ..." The TV went blank. It was a local station. The Malcolms owned it. The airhead commentator was about to expose their links to the drug trade.

DUH!

For all the good that would do. They weren't into drugs or anything else anymore – but they weren't the whole family.

They were the most important part of the family here. Possibly in the states.

Harve called Carter, who answered on the ninth ring. "What the hell! What's going on up there, Harve? Why call me ... oh! You're coming today?"

"No, Cart. The Malcolm family was virtually wiped out last night, along with your favorite judge, Evans. The Malcolms own half of that island. They're probably using it as a drug transfer station. Can you sort of keep an eye on the airport and marina? I'll get there as fast as I can. I think I know who's behind this, here – beside me."

"You? You killed off the Malcolms and *dear* Judge Evans? Gimme a break! You definitely wanted to, but you didn't."

"No. I did say something that set it up. I didn't mean for them to get sliced up, but I'm not really sorry they did. It makes the world a better place."

"Sliced up?"

"Machetes or big knives."

"Being a black Mexican sort of leaves me wondering if some of my people finally had enough shit from that bunch. Sorry I wasn't there to help. I *am* a meatcutter, by trade! Was.

"The Gomez family?"

"No comment! Ongoing investigation!"

"You do tend toward a sort of pragmatism."

They both knew all calls were monitored. They knew the flags, so avoided them.

They chatted a few minutes, then Harve got dressed, packed up the police things that weren't personal property to turn in, and headed for the office.

Talk about a confused mess! Vernor was almost in hysterics. The regular officers weren't patrolling, traffic was in a tangle because the special officers were slow in responding to calls, homicide were both at the hotel – and three officers had not reported to work. Harve noted they were the three who had numerous complaints against them for shaking down the Indians and Mexicans.

He asked Annette about them.

"Goins and Hill got the holy living hell beat out of them this morning on the strip. Edwards seems to have packed up and left town. Jillian went to his place and it was cleaned out and the key was hanging in the door.

"Some reporter said he was going to release a video of some sort. Cappy (She was the only one who called Vernor anything but "Captain Vernor, Sir!") actually pissed in his pants, so I suppose it's something about him running around on Louise, but everyone already knows that. Maybe he doesn't want it on the news, and now Old Man Malcolm isn't here to stop it.

"It's a gawdawful mess."

"Had to happen, sooner or later."

"I guess."

He went into homicide, checked his desk, grinned at the envelope in his "In" basket, lifted it out and read it. It wasn't far from a threat if he ever told anyone anything confidential about the department, and would he please reconsider his resignation? He would receive no positive recommendation if he quit under present circumstances.

There was a lot of noise from out front, so he looked out to see this morning's reporter, Glen Forbes, confronting Vernor, who was almost pleading. He looked very pasty and sick. Harve got an evil smirk on his face and took the note out to innocently ask for a moment of Vernor's time.

"*Now*!? I can't, er, that is, what is it about, officer?"

"I got this letter this morning in my inbox. I don't quite understand what you mean by it? I would never reveal confidential departmental ... things!"

"Er, I don't have time to, I mean, it was the shock, that is, uh, of, er, you see. We don't want you to leave. You're very, uh, that is, you see. Needed. Here. You are the, uh, that is. Best. Investigator, that is, in, uh. Like that kind of, er, thing. You. See."

"Captain Vernor, sir, the investigations were never acted upon, except in a few cases that didn't involve certain families. If a case was secured and certain, evidence would be lost or destroyed and witnesses would refuse to appear. I have no value to such a system. I have no options. I have to find a place where what I work my ass off to find means something. It's not here."

"Detective Plains! I admit there was a great deal of intimidation and just plain crookedness in the system here! I have tried fighting against the powers that ... were ... here! I had to consider the safety of my own people, and we were dealing with suspected drug cartels who had armies we couldn't fight! I have kept very careful records for use by the federal government in prosecuting these violent, vile criminals!

"The Malcolm family, as you are aware, met their deserved fate last night! I can, at last, present my evidence to the federal government!

"The way I see it, the demonstration in the Lowtow ... er, Latino community came at a time when another cartel made a raid, or such. It was supposed to, was set up to, look like the Latinos here, who very definitely and obviously had ample reason, did it, er, you see.

"That didn't work, because of the demonstration, where all the Wetbuh ... er, Latinos, as such, were on camera by our own TV station!

"I can now make an intense and thorough investigation of the drug cartel's actions here! I want *you* to lead that investigation!"

Harve almost laughed in his face. The overdone posing and political posturing were almost comical.

"I'm afraid I've already committed myself to another position (Vernor looked very relieved), so have to decline."

"Well, Officer Plains, we will certainly miss your expert leadership in this, but I would never stand in the way of *any* person being able to better himself!"

"But I have a complete record of all my investigations of the Malcolm family members on memory sticks, including all orders and such. As you know, I record all such things to be able to refer to them if I forget something. I'll get them for you. The TV reporters can vouch for that, showing how much you were following police procedures to bring them to justice, all along."

Vernor swayed. Annette, who had come up beside him during the interchange, caught him, or he would have fainted dead away.

Harve smirked to himself as he went to his desk and came back with a sack of memory sticks, which he handed Forbes. Harve said that was to show that he actually did give all his evidence to Captain Vernor.

"I see it is nearly noon. I have to go home and pack. I'm off to the Caribbean – and it's not running to a paid vacation to avoid testifying! All my testimony is on those twelve four gig memory sticks! They're in a sealed evidence bag, so you can arrange for witnesses to be present when it's unsealed, which is authentication. The dates are on the sticks, so you can see there has been no gap, except two weeks in June of last year, when I was on vacation.

"I'll miss this place and the people here. I wish you well. I'll visit whenever I can."

He waved and walked out. Forbes winked at him and gave him a thumbs up.

Harve made his breakfast, pancakes with strawberry jam, coffee, and a slice of baked ham. He had spent yesterday afternoon packing what he would take along. He would put most of it in storage. In Austin. He didn't believe for a picosecond that something wouldn't happen to it if it was here.

Several people came to talk to him during the afternoon. Vernor came late, with Annette. He wanted to know exactly what was on the memory sticks. Harve said only what had actually happened and been said and done.

"I'm worried that certain departmental issues are discussed on them that would affect the workings of my department," Vernor said, in a slightly threatening way. "I was able to postpone opening the bag until Monday, when we can have state observers present. Federal, if we can get them. I must see that certain people are protected, if you know what I mean. People who you might have mentioned who know too much, or something."

"I'm aware that we had to use a certain discretion. After all, what good would a surprise raid be if someone told about it beforehand? I only recorded official things for my own use, basically, but the Malcolms getting offed like that caused a little change of thought, because it's as plain as day that hard questions are going to be asked. I want it known, beyond doubt, that I was never involved in any way with those cheap thugs, except in investigating them."

Harve knew full well that Annette was recording the whole thing. He was being careful with what he said. Vernor was trying to get something that would discredit him if what was on those memory sticks was what was on those memory sticks.

Wasn't gonna happen, Charlie!

"Well, I worry that someone else in that cartel will think you have evidence or something. It could be very dangerous if certain things were known," Vernor said smoothly. "You are dealing with very dangerous people, after all."

"It would be on the memory sticks, so would be negative to anything that may come up against them if I were to be attacked in any way," Harve replied easily. "That would be too obvious. People are already full to the ears with the bullshit from all of those people. Six or eight of them, no problem. Handle it like always. There comes a point where it's six or eight hundred people, or six or eight thousand, like at the protest, and their power is gone.

"I wouldn't know what might be on those sticks from the past, the only chance any of that bunch has is to get away from anywhere they could be tagged and prosecuted.

"My theory about the Malcolms is that that's exactly what happened. They crossed the line and didn't have sense enough to run to where they couldn't be touched, which *damned* well isn't anywhere around here! Cross the line and there's no going back."

It went like that for about half an hour. Every point Vernor brought up, Harve shot down. If anything happened to him, it was obvious where it came from on the memories. He was a reluctant hero. The outrage wouldn't be "contained."

Harve wouldn't bat an eye if Vernor was suddenly not around tomorrow, having a family emergency somewhere else or something as transparent. He wasn't exactly the brightest star in the galaxy.

Annette looked a lot more worried than Vernor when they left. Why? She hadn't said much – except to bring up a point or two.

Harve looked thoughtful, then went to his computer. It still had the police web codes, so he checked on her.

Annette Grace Birns, daughter of Frederick

Daren Birns and Florence Maebelle (nee Collins) Birns. Normal school and high school. Police department secretary since high school, starting under Captain Donald Reese, then with Vernor for the past nine years.

Not much.

Father F. D. Birns, grandfather, Allen Randolph Birns, mother Agatha Anne Malcolm .... there it was. She was the power controlling Vernor, all along. She was why nothing was prosecuted against the Malcolms.

Harve thought about it, then smirked to himself. Glen Forbes was coming over later. He would leave a time bomb with him when they went for lunch, Glen's treat.

"Well! You certainly put a scare, more a terror, on Vernor!" Glen said, leaning back in the chair to sip his coffee. "I wouldn't be at all surprised if he has something come up that means he has to be out of town on Monday, so we will have to wait to review the memory sticks, heh, heh, sorry about that, Old Sock, but these things come up!

"He's probably been head of it all along. He's as corrupt a snake as ever there was."

"Don't jump to conclusions," Harve warned. "I'll show you something when we get back to my place. I expect someone's searching it right now.

They should know a cop isn't going to leave anything around."

"You used memory sticks. They'll format your computer, at the least."

"Expected. Handled." Harve put a hard drive on the table he had in his carry-case. Glen laughed. They chatted for awhile, then headed back to Harve's apartment, where everything looked normal.

Harve went to the back window, looked at it, then grinned.

"What?" from Glen. "They didn't use the door? I could open that one with my pocket knife!"

"But that would be too obvious, and I might have it booby trapped."

"Do you?"

"Sorta. I expected this." He pointed at the side of the window. Glen didn't see anything. He raised an eyebrow.

"I put a drop of furniture polish on the top. It's not there, but a streak is on the side, showing the window was opened all the way."

He flipped on the computer. Things looked normal.

He went to the registry temps.

"Everything on it was opened. It's another hard drive that didn't *have* anything much on it."

He took out four screws, moved the side panel,

dropped out the hard drive and plugged in the one from his case. "The only thing changed on this (holding up the hard drive he'd removed) is the police entry codes are disabled.

He went to the police web and brought up Annette's file. Glen raised the eyebrow again.

"You figure it out," Harve said. "I want it to appear you found it, or someone else, not me. I may need to appear innocent later."

Glen studied the couple of paragraphs, then scrolled to the one about her father.

"I'll be damned! Two and two! She's a Malcolm, and was there before Vernor, so she's the PIC, all along!"

"And now she's out in the cold, with only one person who can tag her ass!"

Glen grabbed the phone to call the station. He said to get constant surveillance on Vernor. He would be there as soon as possible.

He gave a few orders, then said, "Harve, he went into his private little poolhouse two hours ago. They've kept close surveillance, even without my suggestion. No one's gone in there except Birns, and she stayed for a total of six minutes. She then went out, got into her Lexus, and drove away. The phone's not being answered in the poolhouse.

"We should have caught on a long time ago that a secretary in a police station couldn't afford a damned Lexus!"

"I don't think I want to know anything more about Vernor or Annette or any of the rest of them," Harve said sourly. "I intend leaving here tomorrow. I can't be tied up in this crap!

"You have everything on the memory sticks, and you have who she is, so the fact there was constant watch, that Vernor had no other visitors from when he went in until you found the body means you don't need me, okay?"

"Yeah, okay, Harve. Malcolms owned the TV station, but they can't intimidate or bribe me. I don't know about the others working there, about the watchers. They might have a memory lapse or something."

Harve grinned and snapped the cassette from the phone recorder. "But you have the report, right here, where they said no one else went in there. This is voicecoder quality, so a memory lapse could end them up with charges.

"Glen, this is drugs. You can get the feds here in a blink, and they'll handle the investigation. With the really big Malcolms out of it, they'll go after what's left to try to make themselves seem the heroes. Don't disappoint them until after it's done, then release a documentary that shows what really happened."

"Good point! You'll be out of it, and nowhere

they can scare you, if they're even stupid enough to try."

"To tell the truth, I think I'll still be in it. The main reason I don't want more connection here than I already have is that knowing it would put me into an impossible spot, rather than a slightly dangerous one.

"Ever heard of Isla Tinta Verde?"

"A little. My wife's sister is married to a man from that part of the Caribbean. He says the place is hell that looks like heaven, and that the devil lives there. I think she saw someone from there and told him about it, or something."

"You're not the first to say that to me. I think I'll practice a few things before I go, other than my lousy Spanish.

"Malcolms own more than half the island."

"Practice? Things?"

"Karate, gun slinging. That kind of thing."

"Oh, right. You won the fast draw and accuracy two years running at the rodeo, and you have a black belt or something."

"Second degree. I'm working on third, but I don't think there'll be much competition there – except they might have watched a lot of those silly movies and learned some. It won't be a lot, and any one of those kicks or chops will kill. You don't spin around and deliver the same thing on your opponent. You're unconscious, at best."

"Yeah. Without the choreography, it ain't the best thing to play with. I'll leave you out of it as much as I can. A lot of people saw us together and know I'm here."

"So we went to lunch and I told you I was always suspicious because evidence seemed to evaporate, but I never got what you could call 'solid proof' until this thing with the Gomez family. That case was thrown out, which made my suspicions go up a few hundred degrees."

"Yeah. They the ones who chopped up the lovely Malcolms?"

"Why, Mr. Forbes! I'm shocked! You had them on camera clear across town at the time! I know you couldn't keep them in view every second, seeing there were more than eight hundred people there, but they were part of the community and you *did* see them from time to time!"

Glen grinned. And giggled. "There will never be a way definite proof can be found, I guess. I would, personally, not bother trying. If anyone ever had a good reason to take the law into their own hands, it was there! I saw the bodies. It was as horrible as anything I've ever seen, and I've been on the front in two war zones.

"Well, I guess I'll call on Captain Vernor to get his take on who might be involved in the *rampant* corruption in the local justice (gag) system. I'm sure he will have a good bit to say about how it was never *him*!"

Harve gave him the bird.

"Harve? Glen Forbes here. I'm at the poolhouse at Captain Vernor's place with the state police.

"I'm sure you will recall that I called from your place to ask about him, and that I was told he was in his poolhouse and had received only one visitor.

"I came directly from your place to here to ask him about some of the things that came up because of your computer memory sticks that are to be investigated Monday.

"I could not get a response, so took it on my own authority to enter the poolhouse, as I was expected, so had permission, legally.

"I found him here, dead. They don't yet know how he died, but the forensics team – Judy says to tell you she's on it and ... what? Okay, that it seems to be some fast poison of a relaxant type, whatever that means ... What? Curare? I've heard of that – she says it looks like curare.

"Harve, there was only one person to come here since he came until I came. Annette Birns, his secretary! I can guarantee she's going to get a very thorough look-at, herself! Judy says there's a dart in the back of his neck ... I'll talk later. It's hectic here, but, this one, there's no way we don't know who killed him. We just have to know why!" He hung up.

So. Harve would know what to say. He would be out of it, except maybe to sign an affidavit about Glen making that call. He would say he got the cassette to him later, or simply not explain. Glen could do that.

He finished his packing and called the movers, then helped load the stuff. It was only a little bit. The storage was paid and the driver knew where to take it.

He checked over the apartment carefully to see there was nothing forgotten, then decided to clean up, go to a decent restaurant, then to the Airport Hotel to get his connecting flight at 6:10 in the morning to Isla Tintada, from which a boat would take him to Isla Tinta Verde. It was all arranged and paid.

He got a knock on the door when he was in the shower (naturally) and called to come on in, he would be out soon.

He expected it would be either the police or, if she wasn't already in custody, Annette.

He got out of the shower, dried and was wrapping the towel around his head when he went into the front room. A dart wouldn't penetrate the towel.

It was two men in dark suits.

"I'll just be a minute. I have to put on some clothes. Being interviewed in a pair of boxers might be sexy to some, but isn't exactly classy."

"You might be sexy to Harry, here, but not to me. I'm Dennis Platt, FBI, as you figured the minute you saw us here."

"You weren't worried it might be Annette Birns out here?"

"Annette? No. Why would ... oh. I knew she was the only one who went into that room and he was offed.

"To tell the truth, the towel would stop any dart. I take some chances, but not that kind."

"You will have to cancel your trip tomorrow."

"No, I won't. And don't try to intimidate me with the big bad FBI. That won't play here, much less Peoria."

"We can cancel your passport." He was grinning. He was just joking.

"For which you would receive international publicity for acting to protect a drug cartel?"

"I doubt you could go that far."

"Want to try?"

Dennis laughed, while Harry looked disgusted.

"Come on! I'm not going to get the good cop – bad cop routine, am I?"

Harry let a small grin escape. "Answer a few questions?"

"Okay. Let me get some clothes on."

He put on the fresh trousers and shirt, shoes, and the rest of it, combed his thick mahogany hair, noted he could use a shave, said to hell with it. He could do that in the morning.

He went back to the front room. The FBI wasn't there, but the door was open. They were sitting on the low wall around the planter.

"Oh. I forgot the furniture is already gone. Shall we go to the cafè at the corner? They have booths, and really good shakes."

Dennis shrugged. Harry said that sounded good to him. Why not coffee?

"Their coffee stinks. Literally, as well as figuratively. I like their vanilla shakes."

They went to Lucille's to sit in a back booth with their shakes.

Dennis said the shake really was good! He hadn't had a shake since he was about sixteen years old!

They talked awhile about the Malcolm Clan, as they were called.

Finally, Harry said, "Harve, what we need is why Vernor was killed. What did he know? It doesn't make any damned sense! Anybody who could connect him, with proof, is dead!"

"Hare, I wondered about that, myself. It has to be something tied into who killed *him*. Nothing else begins to fit. There has to be something that ties Annette's tits in a knot. Maybe it was that she was sleeping with him or something. I just realized that I don't know diddly shit about her. She's the only thing – maybe it doesn't have anything to do with the Malcolms. Maybe it was personal."

"That doesn't fit. Branch is checking on her from the womb to today. There doesn't seem to be any connection to ... anything.

"We would have Vernor in a position where he had no choice but to spill his guts. There just has to be something about that in this pile of horse manure we're sifting through."

Harve's cell buzzed. It was Glen. He punched "answer" and said, "Guys, give me a sec. It's a friend.

"Yo, Glen! What's up?"

"I'm talking with some FBI agents right now." Glen asked if this was a bad time. That would tell him to just let Harve handle it.

"You did? What?"

"She is? Really? How did you find that out?"

"Yeah, I guess the station would have access to that kind of thing. Maybe better than the police web."

"Her grandfather was *what*!?"

He turned to Harry and said, "Annette's grandfather on his father's side was married to a Malcolm. That seems to have it pegged, would you say?" Then into the phone, "You checked it ... I see. That was another thing I knew that I never questioned.

"Look. I'll call you later ... how about a couple of beers before I run off into the sunrise?"

He rang off.

"What did you know and didn't consider?" Dennis asked.

"That a secretary in a police station was driving a fifty thousand dollar Lexus."

Harry slapped his head. Dennis rolled his eyes.

"So! She was the king ... or I should say, queen pin all the time?" Harry said sourly.

"It would seem. You don't need me for anything else with that bit of information."

"Guess not. Thanks! I think I really do like you," Dennis said. "Not to the extent I think you're sexy in boxers, though."

"And Harry?"

Harry grinned. "Depends on which end of the stick I'm on."

They chatted and joked for a few minutes, then left. Harve called Glen and agreed to meet him later for a few beers and chuckles.

Harve answered the wake-up call and rolled out of bed. Yesterday was moving day from his apartment. Today was moving day from the states.

He called Cart to tell him he'd get in on the afternoon boat from Isla Tintada. He talked a little about the FBI and what they knew.

"Well, the things you told me to watch for seem to be busy. Lots of excitement. I'd say there was a shipment of farm tools or something that didn't have a destination anymore. They have to get it on its way from here, but they don't have anyplace to send it, and it spoils or something on the order," Cart reported.

"Farm tools that spoil?"

"Picture a fist with the middle finger standing boldly extended."

They joked a minute. Harve went to the restaurant for breakfast, then across to the airport to check in for his flight. The trip to Isla Tintada was smooth and pleasant, if the search and such weren't. He was just in time for the boat to Isla Tinta Verde. He got on the boat as a man he'd seen in the hotel, restaurant, flight to Tintada, now the boat got on. He waved for him to come over.

"FBI, CIA, PI, or a thug for some drug cartel I seem to have exposed when I didn't know anything about them?"

"I'm new at more than local things, like looking for a cheating SOB or bitch. No, no, yes. I don't know who for, and I was only told to watch you wherever you went.

"How did you make me so easy?"

"What the hell! No matter where I looked, there you were!"

"Well, I get to come here, and it really is as good as the pictures, ain't it? Lots of palm trees and oceans and all. I hope the chicks are as hot as in those travel posters!

"I'm Will Walters. Macon, originally."

They chatted. Harve wasn't fooled by this one. Not for a second.

Cart was waiting when they got off the boat. Harve introduced Will. They went to a little local restaurant for a late lunch, then Cart took Harve to a small hotel, where he was soon moved in and comfortable. The place was booked, so Will had to find a place elsewhere. That might be a problem, because there weren't any other hotels. Very few tourists went to Tinta Verde.

Will finally found the one taxi in town and was going to see if the only other place with more than fifty people had a hotel or whatever. It was a couple of miles along the South Road.

When they were, at last, alone, Cart caught Harve up to date on what had happened, and vice versa. They strolled down to the beautiful beach, where only a few locals were wandering around.

"I think, seeing who owns most of this, including the hotel, we can't talk in most places," Harve warned. "Even here, don't move your lips much when you speak."

"Harve, that Will character can only be from two places. If he can't find a place here, it's the FBI or CIA or whatever. If he can, it's from Malcolms."

"I know. That's why I wasted so much time before I came here. If he ends up with a place close by, it's Malcolm." Cart nodded.

"What have you learned about the drug shipment with no destination?"

"They found a destination. I suppose somebody got a great discount deal on a store closing sale." Cart grimaced. "They transferred it to a truck and drove it off on the North Road. That means it has to go from the Shell Point dock. There's nothing else here.

"It's a big risk for them. They almost never move anything from there, because they know it's watched. They've sent decoys to test it, and they were stopped. I think they feel the DEA and coast guard won't check this one because there's never been anything on the any of the ones they've stopped, so they haven't stopped any for awhile.

"It's a risk they shouldn't have taken."

"That could be bad for us. I show up, coming from the place their store went down, then a port that isn't usually checked ... Cart! They must *not* stop that boat! Can you stop them?"

Cart took his cell phone from his pocket and punched a number.

"Elena? Look, I know it's short notice, and I hope I'm not too late, but I can't make it tonight. Not yet. I have a friend from back home visiting, and it's damned important to me to spend some time ... you know.

"You understand, don't you? I don't want to get on your bad side, but, well, old friends are old friends."

"Yeah. It's like that. We can get together later, as soon as I know it won't screw up an old friendship."

"Thanks. I'll call you again as soon as I know for sure it won't cause problems."

"Love ya. I'll call."

He turned to Harve. "Stopped, just in time. The boat's about ready to go out with a load of pineapples. They have a big farm inland a bit.

"They took the stuff there, so when will it go?"

"Any other boats at the dock?"

"Nothing with the range to take anything anywhere."

"They're watching satellite?"

"I suppose. I don't know much about them, but I gave a guy some information about some stuff and I've worked with them since with the harder stuff. You know me. Mild recreational, who gives a flying shit? Addicting trade crap, I want stopped."

Harve nodded. He had always been against criminalizing people for use of pot or such. Even coke, without the crack or other manufactured additives. There were enough actual crimes going on that such things merely complicated.

They strolled along a bit, then headed back to the hotel. It seemed there had been an emergency and a tenant had to leave, so Will could get a room!

"Really? How did you get the news to him, seeing that he had gone to Pearltown?" Harve asked innocently. "He seems to have good luck! Wish I had half as much. If Cart hadn't gotten me my room before I got here, I'd end up sleeping under a palm tree!"

"The no-see-ems would have a feast on you," Cart said. "I'll go to my place and clean up, such as we do here, and meet you in about an hour. I'll show you around. There are some good people here, but there are some of the lowest slime in the world, at the same time."

They agreed on that. Harve went to his room, cleaned up and put on fresh clothes. Cart had warned him to wear long trousers and long sleeves – and to use a Deet cream on all exposed areas. The no-see-ems wouldn't be bad if the breeze held up, but would carry him away if it stopped.

He read some stuff he had with him while waiting for Cart to come.

Will came to knock on his door and say he had

lucked out! The taxi, such as it was, that took him to Pearltown had carried one of the people at the hotel to catch the late boat, and they had a room!

Now, how did you know exactly what to say about a question I only asked in passing where only three employees of the hotel could hear, hmm?

He said he was getting ready to go out, but that it was with Cart, and he didn't know if the plans could include any others. Cart may have arranged company, and bringing in an extra might be a bad idea.

Will said he understood. He'd met a girl he would spend some time with.

Really? When you haven't been here more than twenty minutes? And eighteen of that was moving your stuff into your room?

"That will work out pretty good, then. I'll probably see you around tomorrow."

Will left.

Amateur! And incompetent on top of it!

Cart called and said it would be about half an hour. Something had come up.

He went out to the little bar and had a beer. Cart showed up forty minutes later. They went to a little restaurant a bit inland, where the food was exceptionally good, to Harve, but Cart said it was a little better than average and was large portions.

Cart was six three and built "like Mr. Universe," according to a few of their women friends. He ate a lot.

When they were alone later, waiting for the waitress, Rita, to get off work, Cart said the two smaller boats had loaded packages and started around the island, then went a couple of miles offshore to meet a trawler that was heading back to New Orleans. It would be watched by satellite and stopped as soon as it reached US waters. It would look entirely random.

Irena, Cart's girlfriend, knew a beautiful girl who liked to party once in awhile, so they went to a cantina, had a great time, then to bed.

It was a great night. Balbina was an intelligent and funloving woman who spoke fairly good English. With his little Spanish, Harve had no trouble communicating.

Balbina had to go to work at the export office, while Rita had to shop for vegetables for the restaurant. Harve and Cart decided to stroll along the beach, taking pictures. It would probably take all day, because they would go all the way around, about twelve miles. Betina, the woman at the front desk (a table outside her room door) of the hotel, asked why in the world they would do anything that boring.

"It's boring to you, because you live here. I'm

from a place where the only water we see is in the town swimming pool or in the little creek they call a river," Harve replied. "The only palm trees or seashells or driftwood or a hundred other things I've seen are in pictures – so I'll take a few myself! I never believed those pictures before, but, well, here it is!

"If you were to go to west Texas, you'd be out there, taking pictures of a *real* desert! The tumble weeds and sandstone formations and Gila Monsters would fascinate you!"

"I guess that's right, wot, Mon?! I ain't never seed nuttin like that!"

They took a canteen of water apiece. Cart said they could pick something if they got hungry. They started out.

"We'll get pictures of all the Malcolm stuff. All that amazing tropical island scenery." Cart had been there for several months, so would be the indulgent friend while his old buddy was the enthusiastic tourist. The Malcolms would be suspicious, but wouldn't have any real reason to think it was anything more, except the coincidence of what happened in the states and him coming there at just that particular time. The New Orleans trawler getting stopped tomorrow morning early would add to it, but that would also be iffy to an extreme.

About an hour later, as they were approaching the Shell Point docks, Harve started laughing. Cart asked what was going on.

"Will has been following us since we left the hotel. He's about a quarter mile back along the shore. We're walking near the water, where the sand's wet and compacted. He's staying close to the plants, above the high water line, where it's soft sand."

Cart laughed. "Like walking through drifted snow! He should be worn down enough now to pass out. He isn't in bad shape, but not good, either. I almost feel sorry for him. He's just a schnook doing a job."

"I don't think so. I really don't."

Cart raised an eyebrow. Harve said, "We'll wait and see."

"What?"

"Would the Malcolms hire a total incompetent, considering their long term involvement in their profession?"

"I wondered about that. Who is he, and what...?"

"That also makes me wonder. Mightily. I wonder what we've gotten ourselves into. I wonder why Will didn't give a shit that I spotted him, and I wonder why he's so chatty, and I wonder ... oh, for pity's sake!"

"What?"

"You know the people back in Fairfield. Who, considering what's happened recently, wouldn't know anything about this kind of crap, but who would want to...."

"*Protect* you! The Gomez family – or anyone else in Lowtown! Will looks like a Latino mix. He's the only one they knew anything about at all they could get to protect you!"

"It struck me from the first that there was something familiar about him. He has a lot of the Vallardes family traits. The ears and the nose, particularly." Harve turned and waved to Will, who came down to the beach and came to them.

"We took pity on you, wading through that sand. You might as well walk with us," Cart said. "We spotted you as Wilam Vallardes from the first minute. We really do appreciate the idea, but Harve can take care of himself."

Will grinned sheepishly. "I thought he probably had spotted me and knew who I am. I'm here because I was once on this island and know a lot about what they're doing here. I *am* a sort of private eye. Learning, anyhow. Harve is our friend.

"My full name is Omar Wilam. Vallardes is my mother's name. Omar Wilam V. here, but Omar W. Vallardes in Texas.

"Harve, there is a person, besides me, who came

from Fairfield."

"That bookworm type in the back of the plane? I was wondering. He was in Fairfield the last day, day before yesterday. I didn't pay any attention, and wasn't sure he was the one on the plane. His disguise is pretty good – which tells me something, but I don't know what."

"Emilio was right beside him when he came to Fairfield. He met with the Annette woman. She gave him some papers. He didn't have glasses then. When I went to the head in the plane I went past him, and they are just glass.

"He has a gun. On the plane. He is staying on a boat at the marina. He didn't come on the boat with us here."

"How did you get into the hotel?" Cart asked.

"I was here before. I know Madelena, at the hotel. She did something. Nobody here likes the Malcolms. They will help you.

"We have to find out who our other follower is. It'll be FBI – CIA, if he's carrying on a plane," Cart suggested. "I wonder how big this really is. I wonder who else is involved. It's looking more and more like Ollie North and associates."

"Who or what is Ollie North?" Will asked.

"He was a big US Marine back a few years who was working with the CIA to protect drug runners in return for help against the Nicaraguan debacle," Cart replied. "Thanks to that shit, no one has trusted the CIA since, and they *do* tend to fuck up anything they get involved in."

"They're a joke in Mexico and Guatemala, where my tios live," Will said. "He has a gun. Do you? I can probably find one for you."

"I have an arsenal," Cart answered. "I doubt we'll need anything like that, here. We want to keep playing it as low-key as we can. Weaken the Malcolms, then eliminate them.

"Harve, you must have a plan. You always do."

"Sort of a half-assed one. I want to get as much info as possible. These pictures will help. We can attack their assets here. We've already put them in a bad situation that'll affect cash flow. We have to see where they get backing after a few major losses.

"Will, do you have people you can trust, absolutely, here?"

"Absolutely? I think ... one. Two."

"All we'll need is to know who comes here to meet with them, or when they go somewhere else. Where. We can probably trace who, if it's not here, because of where they come from."

"I have family on Tintada. That's where they would meet someone else from somewhere else."

Harve nodded. "We have to use some kind of code to contact them."

"A girl I know goes to Isla Tintada every week. She handles the things they grow here, like the pineapples and avocados and fresh mariscos. She can tell my sobrinos whatever," Will suggested. "She can bring back messages. She did that for us already."

They discussed it more as they walked on. Harve got a lot of pictures.

When they reached Pearltown, an overdressed, suave man came to them on the beach. He said he overheard them speaking English, and he didn't get much practice here.

Oh? You overheard us from a hundred feet away – when we weren't saying much? Cart knew what Harve was thinking. He smirked.

"I'm Harvey, from Texas. I've never been in this kind of place before. Cart is an old friend. He invited me for a vacation. He lives here. Will was on Isla Tintada at a cousin's place. He's from Texas. We sort of ganged up to look over the island. It's really different! I've taken a thousand pictures, at least!"

"Well, yes. It's a tranquil and bonita place. I'm called Eduardo. I have a farm here. I had family in the estados. I was in Texas for two years, where I learned my poor Englsh.

"I found this island had a bad reputation in Texas. I am surprised you would come here for a vacation."

"Oh, you hear that about all the islands. Voodoo and magic curses and a lot of crap," Harve said, with a laugh. "I don't even listen to it. I had a lot of that kind of stuff when I was in New Orleans. I went to Loyola for four years, so know that some of it's scary, but don't cross any of them and you don't have a problem with them. I get along with people pretty good. You don't mess with me, I won't mess with you."

"A very good way to look at the world, it would seem," Eduardo replied. "You don't mess with me, I won't mess with you." There was an obvious threat in the way he said it.

"What the fuck was that!?" Cart snarled. "Who the hell do you think you are? Nobody said anything about messing with you! It looks like you're the one who wants to start something, so take a little lesson. You threaten my friends, you threaten me! It would take me two seconds to break your stupid fucking neck, hijo de puta!"

Eduardo turned and stalked away. There were a couple of big men who had come close.

"What the hell was that about?!" Harve cried. "What a *crud*!"

One of the men started to move toward them. The other grabbed his arm and shook his head. They left.

"What was it about?" Cart asked.

"To see if I was who and what I am, so I acted like I'm just some tourist who can't believe anyone would be such an ass, so I must just be a stupid tourist who doesn't know his ass from a cowflop.

"It was stupid. They *gave* me a reason to investigate them!"

"They seem to be under a lot of pressure, for some reason. They acted too fast and without thinking. Now they can't ever know for sure," Cart said, smirking again. "I wonder what may have happened elsewhere that would make them wonder about us?"

Will didn't know what was happening, and was scared. "That was El Diablo, himself! Madre de dios!"

"El Diablo?" Harve asked.

"Si. Eduardo Malcolm Flores. El Diablo!"

"It would seem you have caught the interest of the head of the clan. Here, at least," Cart said. "Shall we keep his interest?"

"We should maybe increase it a few degrees. We can be under his very close scrutiny while very bad things happen – so we couldn't be behind them, could we?"

"Harve! Cart! He will just have you killed! That way, there will be no problems with you! It is what he does! It is what he is!"

"Then we'll have to de-horn El Diablo, won't we?" Cart suggested.

"Sounds like a plan!"

They went on along the beach around a curve into a small bay to just outside view of the little village, where Harve had them leave the beach and go onto the road. They saw a car that had been in Pearltown parked under some trees ahead.

"Hm. Don't kill us that close to the village. There would be witnesses. Here, there wouldn't be," Cart said. "I wonder if El Diablo is in that car? He might want to watch, but he would never get his hands dirty doing the job." He reached behind his back and brought out a Glock 40, which he handed to Harve. He reached under a trouser leg and brought out an old Luger, grinned, and said it was always his favorite tool.

They stayed under the roadside brush to quietly approach the car. The two goons were in a copse of sea grapes, with rifles, watching the beach.

Cart started toward the goons, but Harve stopped him and mouthed, "Wait." They waited silently for about five minutes. Harve wrote a note on a slip of paper and handed it to Will, who read it, looked very scared, and nodded. He moved to the road and walked toward the car. As he passed it, he was called over to the window, where he spoke for a few seconds, then went on toward the town. The driver of the car stepped out and called for Santos and Guillermo to come to the car. They argued with the driver a minute, then got in the car and headed back toward Pearltown.

"What did Will tell them?" Cart asked.

"Why, that the man from Peru came in a boat and made you get in and they went back around the island and left him there to get back to town as best he could and he was royally pissed about it!"

"Man from Peru?"

"He has to wonder if it's some other cartel, which would explain a lot of their recent troubles – or maybe the same family in a power play? That would *also* explain a lot!"

"You're sneaky!

"What next?"

"Why, we show up in town and aren't saying anything about anybody. We seem to be scared of something or other." He handed the Glock back. "Oh! And by the way, the guy from Peru was the same one who met that nerdy gringo on the boat last night."

"You're somethin' else!"

They laughed and joked as they walked to just before town, then took a side path to the other road to come into town from the other side of the island, it would appear. Cart went to his place and Harve went to the hotel. Eduardo was sitting in the lobby. He wished he'd kept the Glock!

<u>Confusing Scenarios</u>

"Waiting for me?"

Eduardo looked up with a hard stare. Santos and Guillermo came from the hallway to stand there, looking like the goons in the sillier movies. Harve laughed.

"What is so funny?" Eduardo asked. He made it sound like a threat.

"Aren't clowns *supposed* to be funny?"

"There is nothing humorous here!"

"Oh, get a grip! Everything's funny to me! What is this supposed to be? Some kind of candid camera? Don't you need a crew for that?

"I get that crap from you at that little village, I get kidnaped and asked a lot of questions that don't make sense, then I get released and some turkey from the CIA asks me some of the same questions, then I come here and you're here?

"You went too far. It's not scary anymore, it's comical.

"What do you want? I have a date, so make it quick.

"Cart's gonna get a real kick out of this!"

Eduardo seemed totally lost. "Who was the man

from Peru? I must know!"

"Man from ...? Oh. You mean Julio, the one who supposedly kidnaped Cart and me?

"That was overdone. They would have taken Will, too. If they were going to scare me and Cart into telling them some ridiculous totally incomprehensible crap about 'The Product' and who told the coast guard it would be on that ship – about which I don't have a clue and couldn't care less – that was stopped ... I mean, come on! Make it minimally believable!"

"Julio? Julio, er, Averiez?"

Almost slipped up there! You told me who you're scared of!

"Averiez? They only called him Don Julio. His goons weren't as crude as yours. You could maybe fix that for the next time you pull this trick.

"You're the only one who had me fooled with the scary bit. You did that really good, only you look too much like a game show host. Maybe have a Cuban cigar hanging out of your mouth so you fit the stereotype. You talk too smooth. Growl and snarl a lot.

"Cano! That's what the boatman called him. Sr. Cano!"

"Maybe if I knew who all you people are supposed to be, it would work better. Scaring me with people I never heard of won't work, most times."

Eduardo looked like he would faint.

"One thing that you fooled me with for a minute was the CIA turkey. He was about what people think of them as being. Macho little fuckups who don't have a clue or an IQ.

"I really do have a date. Work on your act a little, and don't go quite so far with it, and it could be a real hoot to tell the grandkids how their grandpop had a terrifying experience with the South American mafia or something. Add a voodoo angle, and it could be a scream! A witch woman who cackled and made curses, but don't take that too far, either. The extremes give you away."

He went to his room. Eduardo and the goons didn't seem to know what to do.

Gee! I wonder why you look so confused?

He wondered if anyone was waiting for Cart. *That* would be worth a video!

Actually, he was surprised by his ability not to piss his pants. It really was a very scary experience, particularly because he knew Malcolm was a sadistic killer. He got the shakes as soon as he was in his room.

He was damned well going to get a pistol from Cart.

Make that an AK-47. A fast draw wasn't much good against several of them.

He told Cart what had happened. Cart said two thugs tried to make it look like a mugging when they killed him. One was dead and the other might not survive. Karate wasn't what the movies made it look like. If you get a full kick to the side of the head, it'll break your neck, often as not, and a chop to the throat will break the cartoid bone and you will die.

They went to the same restaurant as the night before. Rita had other plans and Elena had to go to Tintada.

"I can live with it. It's been a stressful day. There aren't many girls here who are unattached," Cart said. "I know a couple of gay guys, but you won't go for that."

"You do?"

Cart shrugged. "They look at it different here. Whatever turns you on. No love or any of that crap. Just fun."

"No thanks." They joked awhile longer, then went to their places for the night. They were both tired.

In the morning, the CIA (or whatever) man was waiting in the hotel restaurant. He asked Harve if he could join him. Harve waved at the other seat at the table.

"No games. What did you say to Eduardo that has my ass in a crack?"

"You? Nothing ... maybe the bit about the CIA man who asked me a bunch of questions after Julio Cano kidnaped me and asked a lot of the same questions."

"Are you for real? Cano kidnaped you?"

"Uh-oh? You're playing both ends against the middle? Sorry.

"Harvey Plains."

"What?"

"I'm Harvey Plains."

"And...? Oh. Lesley Downs. I know who you are.

"Is there a reason I shouldn't slow-roast your ass?" He grinned.

"It would get yours deep fried."

He laughed. "How do we save anything from this mess? We're trying to shut them all down."

"I'll shut this one down. That might get Cano shut down. The others are your problem. This one is personal."

"You won't be the first who's tried."

"No one's tried my way."

They chatted about music and the way it had turned to noise in the states, but was about the same on the islands and steadily improving in the rest of Central and South America, while they enjoyed the meal.

Harve called on Will, who had a pretty, if a bit young, to Harve's way of thinking, girl with him. She kept giving him the eye and licking her lips.

About sixteen or seventeen and an experienced prostitute, by the looks of it.

Will sent her on her way and they talked for about an hour. They made plans, of a sort. Will would be the ignorant schnook who said the wrong thing at the wrong time and didn't have a tiny clue as to what was going on in front of his face.

Next, Cart would be moving around, seeing what there was to see. No one connected him to the two bodies in the alley at Pottertown Road. One had a broken neck, the other had a bullet in the head (!).

"Knew who hired them," Cart explained. "If he lived, he would have talked."

Harve nodded. "Part of the job description."

"What you got planned?"

"I heard about the pineapple farm and wanted to see how they were grown and processed, so I'll take my little camera and walk around the interior, seeing I've seen the beaches."

"Damnit, Harve! Be careful!"

"I damned well will. Can you give me a pistol I can use fast-draw with? A Glock ain't it."

"Yeah. I'll give you a good old Colt thirty eight. It's got a standard holster, but you can cut it for fast-draw. You can carry it here in a holster, and can claim it's for snakes. There are some really bad-ass ones here.

"Harve, please, be damned careful."

"They need me, now. Everything's about to cave in, and I can get information for them I don't know I'm getting. So long as I can make them believe I'm coincidental, but with potential, I'm safe enough."

They talked a bit more, then Harve went to the hotel to get his camera and strap on the Colt. He modified the holster just a little.

He took a deep breath and went out. He wasn't nearly as sure of himself as he was projecting, but it had to be done.

He spoke with a couple of people on the way out of town. He'd met them in the bars with Cart. They were friendly and had good senses of humor. He said he was going to the pineapple farm, they said it was a few hectares of pine-apples. Hooray and whoopie. He said he'd never seen more than a couple in pots before, and wanted to see how they were processed for shipping.

About a kilometer from town he saw he was being followed, or someone else was going to the farm, so he went to the side of the road under a tree to wait for the one Eduardo called Santos to come trotting up.

"Hi. Santos, wasn't it? I'm Harve. It will be easier to follow me if we're together. Maybe you can tell me what the hell's going on."

Santos laughed. "Mon, you got balls! Wot you think?"

"That's the rub. I don't know *what* to think. The act was a lot too much to swallow. I guess it makes my vacation more interesting, but I don't get it. Why?"

"Why?"

"Why the silly big bad gangster act?"

"It ain't no act, mon. Don Eduardo, he in real deep shit with somebody he don't know who. I ain't never seen him scairt afore, but him damn well scairt now! Him act like Mama Bernadette done gone fer his ass, mon!"

"Mama Bernadette? You mean there really is a witch in this mess?"

"Her ain't no witch. Her Doctora Voodoo. Her queen in the islands, mon. No scairt if her get after you ass, you plain stupid!"

"I'm not about to get her or anyone else after my ass. I'm just on my vacation and all of a sudden I'm mixed up with some kind of comedy TV show or something. I guess it should bother me, but I don't know many people here, and everyone's following me, so I can talk to people.

"I like to talk."

He laughed again. "You done cool, mon! You bees glad you don't know from shit 'bout nothin. I done am wishing I don't know nothin.

"Don Eduardo half want me kill you and half scairt'n you. He scairt uhcause Cano asked somethin and you still walkin around. That mean him can't know if you is more than you is.

"I see fun in you. None of those got no fun, Even Guillermo don't got no fun. Life ain't no good lessen you got fun.

"Why you comin out here?"

"I'm from west Texas. We don't have pineapples and avocados and a hundred things. We buy them in cans or at the fruit market. I just want to see what they're like in their natural habitat."

He looked thoughtful, then looked at Harve. "I sposed to kill you."

"Really? Why?"

"I don't know. Don Eduardo say to kill you, I kill you.

"He say if it don't look good, don't do it now. I ain't gonna. You fun, mon. Ain't nobody here fun." They walked on, chatting and making jokes. They came to the pineapple farm, where there were acres of the plants in different stages of growth. Several people were moving along, cutting off the pineapples sticking above the plants and tossing them into a cart behind a tractor. There was a shed ahead where another cart was being unloaded. A panel truck was just beyond. They walked on. The pineapples were cut off the stems and packed in boxes that were sealed, then loaded on the truck.

"The truck takes 'em to the boat. The boat takes 'em to Isla Tintada. A refrigerated container takes 'em up to the states," Santos lectured. "They done green, just startin to yellow. Too yellow, they rot afore they get there. They done got that plant wot put 'em in cans. Make vinegar from scraps. Them boxes to the side is cans. Same truck.

"Now you see pineapples from plant to plant." He grinned.

"It is interesting. In a way, it's more than I thought. In a way, less."

They soon headed back to the town. Harve was sure he'd seen something that would prove interesting to ... whoever. He would have to talk to Les. He did get to where he kind of liked Santos.

Santos would report he didn't know what was going on, and to kill him would mean a bunch would come from the states to ask questions. Too many people knew he was there, and he was a cop in the states, so they would get upset because of that. He would say that cops in the states had specialties, and Harve was a murder cop, so didn't even look at anything else. If he was murdered, a hundred murder cops would want to investigate. They stuck together.

Harve downloaded his pictures and selected a few, then called Cart, who would meet him in half an hour at the restaurant. He called Will, who said he would probably drop by there later. Harve said he might as well bring that CIA guy along (who Will didn't even know, so he would know to contact him and have him there, if possible) so they could all be together and maybe he could find out what the hell was going on. It was getting damned tiresome to be followed everywhere he went.

He went out to find Santos in the lobby.

"You going to be in the line to follow me now?"

He laughed. "Yea, mon! I done tole Don Eduardo you talked a lot and said things you didn't know you said an that we were sort of friends. He say it a good idea. Maybe you say somethin you don't know an it tell him somethin he need to know, an I done got nothin else to do nohow so why not."

"I'm going to dinner and maybe to a bar or two. I can't pay for you. I don't have that much."

"I get five hunderd. Don Eduardo give me what I need. I can pay for all'n us!" He really was likeable. When he wasn't trying to be a hood, he was a fun sort.

They were joking about the teenage girl prostitutes when Cart came up to raise the eyebrow.

"Oh! Cart! This is Santos. He's supposed to kill me if I get out of line or something. He went along with me to the pineapple plant ... plant." He and Santos giggled.

They went to the restaurant, where Will and Les were sitting, talking to a fat woman. She left soon and they pulled two tables together.

The talk was mostly about the women – or lack of same – on the island. They were a big enough bunch that the owner, the fat woman, it turned out, made a special meal for them that was really a special meal. Santos paid for it, almost fifty dollars. Rita joined them. They had a gallon of rum and a 2 liter Coke, so were getting a little high. Harve managed to tell Les to meet him somewhere tomorrow. He had an idea.

Cart and Rita left about midnight. The rest finished the rum and headed their separate ways. Santos went along with Harve. At the hotel, Santos asked if Harve wanted him to stay. He didn't know how to take that.

"You mean?"

"Well, mon. No women an we both horny. Wot's the hell?"

He didn't know what to say. Santos broke out, laughing. "I done need a camera for you face, mon! I forget you from states and think different. I done stayin if you want. It done different here."

Harve laughed. "Damn! I think I'm actually considering it! I've never done anything like that."

Santos cocked his head to the side and grinned.

"Done considering! I'm not ready!"

Santos laughed and said he'd probably see him in the morning. Try to sleep late, because he probably would.

Harve went to his room and flopped on the bed. The next thing he knew, he was waking up to birds singing and the sun coming in his window.

He went to breakfast. Santos came in before he finished, so he bought the same for him. They joked all through it.

"Wot you do today, mon? No long walkin til after lunch, okay? I done got a little hangon. Hang ... over?"

"Me, too. Just a little. It'll be alright in an hour or so. I'm just going to hang around and maybe read a book. I might go sit by the beach.

"Say! I saw a guy fishing on the beach yesterday! Can you catch anything in the surf here?"

"Yea. You got some good fish here. I got some stuff. I fish some, most to get away from ... things."

Harve said he would be right there for awhile, so Santos would get him some fishing equipment. He would like to fish, too.

Cart came in a few minutes after Santos left. He said he didn't know if Harve should trust Santos. Harve said that was true, at first, but he could now.

There were some pictures and a few suggestions he wanted to get to Les, but it had to look like something innocent. Cart said he would arrange something. They could be right there in front of Santos and he wouldn't get a clue.

He got his camera, downloaded everything on his computer, then put several pictures, those taken at the pineapple farm, on the camera. It would look like he had put in a new card for that.

Santos came back with some rods and reels. Harve said he didn't think that heavy a rod and reel would be used in surf fishing! All he ever saw was some light stuff for in the river that was actually no more than a creek.

They went to the surf. Santos caught a few sand crabs for bait, and they cast into the rolling small waves.

He got a strike almost immediately. He brought

in a ... catfish? What they called a sail cat. He'd heard they were good to eat.

"Yea. Okay, but give 'em to the kids."

Santos caught a big sting ray, which they threw back. His next strike was mostly a little tug that kept moving and got stronger and stronger.

"Shark, mon. Less you wants the fight, cut it loose."

He didn't want the fight. "Not with a shark, if half the tales I've heard are true."

"They probably ain't, but I done would cut it."

He cut the line. He was trying to stop it, but hardly slowed it.

Cart and Will came strolling along the beach. They stopped to chat. Harve had his camera in the case and said he'd seen the pineapple farm yesterday. It was kind of interesting. He had pictures still in the camera.

Cart rolled his eyes and Will said maybe some, just to see what it was like. He hadn't gone inland that far.

Harve showed them the pictures on the screen, managing to tap the screen on several, one where they were loading the truck he tapped a couple of times, the last on the stack of boxes from the canning plant.

He put the camera back and slipped out the mini-memory chip, which he slipped to Will when

Santos got a strike. He brought in the large wahoo. Harve took several pictures, including a short video just as they beached the fish.

"Now, that is a good one to eat! I can have Ronda fix it and cena done be on me again!" Santos announced proudly. "No rum after! Once a month done be too much!"

They laughed and joked. Harve caught a large black bass, and they went their ways, he and Santos back to the hotel, where Santos told the cocinera (cook), the aforementioned Ronda, to fix a meal for six or eight with it. Seven o`clock. She would put the bass in the freezer for later.

Harve said he was tired. He was going to do something he never did. He was going to take a nap! Santos said that was perfect. He would, too!

They went to Harve's rooms. Harve went into the bedroom and said Santos could use the fold-out sofa. Santos got a whipped puppy look, and said, "Awww." They laughed.

Harve stripped to his jockeys and laid on the bed with the fan on him. Santos stripped and laid on the fold-out with another fan on him.

[Will took the mini-memory chip to Les to place in the adaptor, then into the slot on the computer. It had a .rtf document, which he read quickly.

A) pineapples being boxed. Note background:

box for overripe for canning plant. Very few.

B) boxes being stacked for truck. Note boxes far right from canning plant. Note the number.

C) pineapples being loaded into truck. Note lower left boxes. They are loaded last, so will be first taken out of truck.

Conclusion: the drugs you couldn't find the distribution system or how they were gotten off the island. – very few for canning plant – quantity of cans, consider part is made into vinegar – cans are in back of truck.

Perhaps, when the boxes are being unloaded an accident that would damage a few of those boxes to where one was broken open?

Will smirked. They only missed what was too obvious to miss. Harve hadn't missed it.

Les got out his scrambled/coded phone and made a call.]

Harve got up and went into the sala. Santos was asleep, looking like an innocent child, in a way.

He was an experienced killer, but also a lot of fun, and honest.

Harve went to the bath and took a long, cool shower, shaved and combed his slightly wild hair. He was standing there, nude, looking at himself in the mirror.

He was no movie star, but not bad-looking.

Maybe a little better than average. He was toned and in shape.

"Pretty good," Santos said from the doorway. "Sort of sexy.

"Ready yet?"

Harve blushed. "No. I have to say you aren't bad at all. It's just not my thing."

"Bet, if I raped you, you's think different! I could rape you, then you could rape me!"

They joked a bit, then dressed and went out to the lobby. There was a bullish, dark man and three obvious thugs there. Cart was over to the side. He mouthed, "Cano."

"Yeeee!" Santos cried.

"Hello! Julio, isn't it?" Harve said brightly. "Surely, you aren't going on with this overdone act?"

Will came in the side door and moved to behind two of the goons. Cart moved behind the other.

Cano sneered. "Naldo, you will teach Mr. Plains a lesson in respect!" he ordered.

One of the goons stepped toward Harve – and found himself flat on the floor with Cart's foot on his neck. Will was joined by Les, from somewhere, to cover the other two goons with pistols.

"Santos, enseñar Sr, Canos un lección en respeta!" Harve ordered.

"Yeeee!" Santos cried. Cano looked just short of terrified.

"Now! If we're through with the bullshit badass crap, what do you want?" Harve asked. "I've had all the cheap theatricals I care to put up with. Make it short. I'm the impatient type."

"You have made the mistake! I will pull the roots! No one closer than second cousin in your family will be alive this hour tomorrow!" Cano screamed.

"Well, I'm an orphan, so I don't know anyone closer than me in my family, so have a go at it.

"You are assuming, of course, that it won't be you who gets the roots pulled. You're hardly in a position to make that decision, at the moment.

Naldo suddenly tried to twist and grab Cart's leg. He got his head bounced off the tile floor, hard, for his effort. Cano squealed.

"Big bad jefe!" Cart snarled. "So long as you have three or four goons to back up what you say. You don't have the gonads to do anything for yourself."

"You will pay! You will see!"

A boy ran out from the hallway, screaming, "Ronda! Los hijos de putas matar Ronda!"

Cart ran toward the hall. Will smacked the goon he was behind on the head with the butt of his pistol. Hard! Les grabbed the hair of his goon.

Santos stood in shock for a couple of seconds, then stepped in front of Cano, said, "Bastard cheap son of a bitch motherfucker!" and stabbed him in the chest with a switchblade stiletto. He was bent over and gasping. Santos stabbed him again, and again.

Cart came back in. "She was raped and her throat cut."

He went to the still-conscious goon Les was holding. His arm snapped out and the goon dropped, gasping. It was too fast to see. Cart spun and delivered a very hard kick to the groin. The goon squealed and folded over into a fetal position, retching.

There was blood running from the nose of the one Will had hit. The one Cart had dropped was just regaining consciousness. He saw what had happened and lunged at Cart, who kicked him hard in the face, snapping his head back. They heard the neck break.

"I think, just perhaps, the Cano Cartel is suddenly out of offshore business," Les said. "I hope they don't get the idea that someone here is making a power play. It could get bloody in several countries."

They stood looking around. Two local police officers, such as they were, came running in, guns drawn, to stand staring at the scene.

"My friends and I came here for a conference in the dining room and found this *horrible* mess, that was *obviously* the result of some kind of drug deal, seeing the internationally known Sr. Cano was involved!

"This is the most *horrible* thing I have ever *seen*!" Les cried.

One of the cops saw Santos standing there, looking lost. He asked something in Patoi, which Santos, who still had the knife in his hand, answered. "El Jefe" and "Mr. M." were mentioned.

That cop ran back out.

"I told him they tried to get me to kill Don Eduardo and someone I don't know came with a friend and we turned it around on 'em. He'll warn El Jefe to get ready for war.

"Ronda was my sister."

"They have to shut this up to protect Malcolm. I don't think I want to be on this island in about six hours. It's going to get very *very* damned hairy," Les suggested.

"I sort of think I want to go to Tintada," Cart said. "I'll visit there awhile. I think there may be someone else here from Cano. It can be dangerous."

"Someone else? What?" Will asked.

"Oh, it's not logical that Cano would be here

alone. Not if he was planning to take out Malcolm. It's part of the way they operate. He would want to keep control for himself, but to send a lesson to anyone who would resist him."

Les looked suspicious. "What do you mean?"

"Well, say their processing plant had an accident? It would be a thing that could be fixed pretty fast."

"An accident?"

"Uh-huh. Like, maybe „„," He took out his cellular and punched a number. They could feel a bit of a shake and concussion. "... maybe a fifty gallon drum of ether got a spark or something. That stuff's volatile as hell, and damned dangerous!

"Don't look at me like that, Harve. I made sure the regular workers there were far enough away that they wouldn't be hurt.

"Exit this branch of the Malcolm Enterprises or whatever."

"Well, now it will be a vendetta among the families in Peru and Colombia, mostly. There are already a lot of them fighting among themselves. They have to stop pot being legalized, like in Uruguay, before it puts them out of business.

"Shall we go somewhere else? This is rather depressing, what? Old Chap!"

Santos said he couldn't just leave like that.

"Santos, you're my friend. It's done here. Nothing can change that. If I ever thought there was any possibility any innocent person would be hurt, I would have done it differently.

"I know that's not much comfort, but you did pay the hijo de puta back in coin."

Santos nodded. Harve Put his arm a round his shoulders. He turned and buried his face in Harve's chest, hugged him, and stepped back.

"You are the only real friend I ever had."

They left. The cop was alone. They went to their places, then to the dock as a group, got on Les's boat, and headed for Isla Tintada.

Harve leaned back on the chaise lounge and sipped his tequila and grapefruit juice. Cart came from the next room with a beautiful girl, patted her on the ass, and she went on into the hotel lobby.

"Just saw on the TV from the states, CBS from Denver. A woman who was connection with a drug cartel and a police department in Texas, Annette Birns, was convicted of murder one. Life without.

"You heard the bit last night where two large drug cartels had a war going on for control of both had decimated each other to where the USDEA had no trouble shutting them both down."

"Yeah," Harve replied. "Will e-mailed that he was back, that the Gomez family wanted me back to be police chief, and that he hoped he never had anything like that again in his life. He never knew what was going on and was so scared he couldn't move, half the time."

"You goin' back?"

"No. I have an offer for a job, chief and police

department on some little paradise island. Tinted Birds? Something like that. I think I'll take it. It'll be like retirement. I'll retire at twenty eight."

"Santos seduce you yet?" Santos had just come from the hotel. They were on Isla Tintada.

"I will! You'll see!" They all laughed.

"Santos, do you want a job? I know you're recently unemployed," Harve asked.

"A yob? Wot, mon?"

"Chief deputy for the Isla Tinta Verde police department."

"Serio?"

"Si."

"Okay. I done be close. I done can seduce you easy, mon."

"That's the idea, I think!" Cart said.

They all laughed. They spent most of the rest of the day walking around the island and meeting people. Harve was introduced to a beautiful sexy woman, Estrella Vasquez, and spent the evening and night with her. In the morning they packed what little they had and headed back to Isla Tinta Verde. Just before they left for the island, Harve got an e-mail; *Les is Moore now! Going to Costa Rica. Best. BTW, you are now titled owner of all assets of E. Malcolm on Tinta Verde. You can grow pineapples!*

Harve gave the computer the bird.

C. D. Moulton's works are available on most major outlets as printed or e-books. CD writes the CD Grimes, PI, mysteries, the Det. Lt. Nick Storie mysteries, the Clint Faraday mysteries, the Flight of the Maita science fiction series, books on orchid culture and many others of many types. Mystery, adventure, intrigue, science fiction, humor, fantasy, paranormal, mild erotica, and factual.

* 9 7 9 8 2 2 3 7 9 9 0 3 0 *